JANICE N. HARRINGTON
PICTURES BY SHELLEY JACKSON

MELANIE KROUPA BOOKS
Farrar, Straus and Giroux • New York

THE CHICKEN-CHASING QUEEN OF LAMAR COUNTY

In memory of Lillian Pennington
—J.N.H.

For Sean
—S.J.

I'm the Chicken-Chasing Queen of Lamar County.

Big Mama says, "Don't you chase those chickens. If you make those girls crazy, they won't lay eggs. You like eggs, don't you?"

But I don't care. Soon as I wake up, wash away the dreaming, and brush my teeth whiter than a biscuit, I always do three things: eat breakfast, tell stories to Big Mama, and—when Big Mama isn't looking—

CHASE CHICKENS!

I go sneaking up on those chickens real slow, real easy, and then—freeze.

I make myself as still as sunlight. And those chickens hold still, too: one leg raised in the air, just waiting to step off. "Pruck! Pruck!"—which must be chicken for "What's she up to this time?" And then . . .

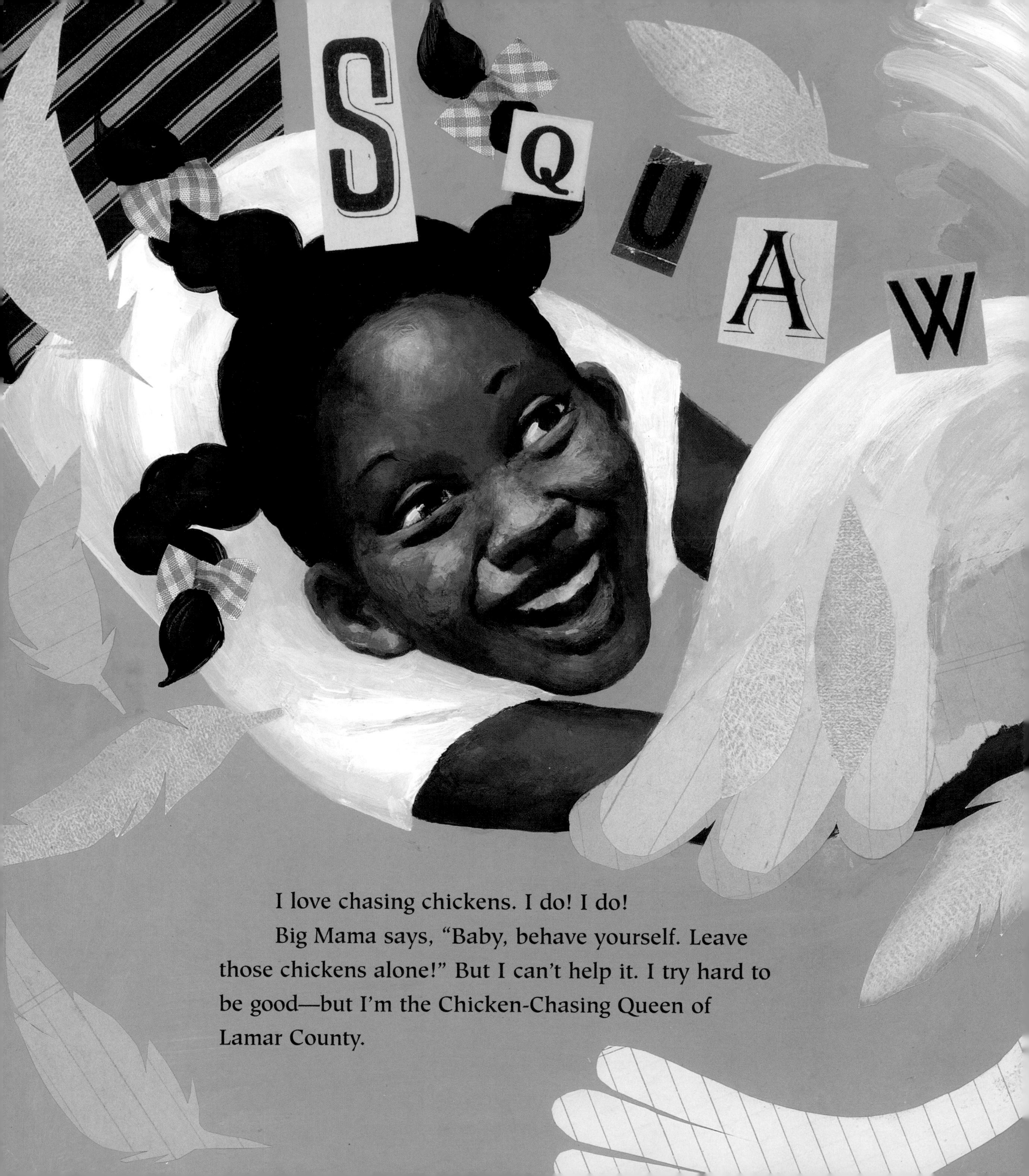

I love chasing chickens. I do! I do!

Big Mama says, "Baby, behave yourself. Leave those chickens alone!" But I can't help it. I try hard to be good—but I'm the Chicken-Chasing Queen of Lamar County.

KKKK!

I don't want just any chicken. I want my favorite. Her feathers are shiny as a rained-on roof. She has high yellow stockings and long-fingered feet, and when she talks—"Pruck! Pruck! Pruck!"—it sounds like pennies falling on a dinner plate. I call her Miss Hen, and she's plump as a Sunday purse—just waiting for me to pick her up.

I never do, though. I never even get close. Miss Hen is fast as a mosquito buzzing and quick as a fleabite.

Miss Hen and I have an understanding. I do my best to catch her, and she does *her* best not to get caught. But just you wait and see. I'm one smart chicken chaser!

This morning I ate breakfast, I told Big Mama stories, and now I'm going after Miss Hen!

Big Mama calls, "Girl, are you chasing those chickens? You know what I told you about that!"

"No, ma'am, I'm not *chasing* chickens."

Nope, this morning, I'm *thinking*. What will I need to catch Miss Hen? Should I take a rope? Nope, Miss Hen's too fast. Should I try some corn bread?

Big Mama says you catch more flies with honey than with vinegar, and I know just what kind of honey Miss Hen likes. When Big Mama isn't looking, I skip all around the yard shimmy-shaking corn bread from my pocket, crumbs falling like a yellow necklace. Then I sneaky-hide behind Big Mama's wheelbarrow and make myself small, small, small.

I don't have to wait long. One by one, Mr. Rooster and the chicken ladies come stepping by. Peckity-scratch-peck. Peckity-scratch-peck. Beaks down and bottoms up. Chickens clucking, squabble-squawking. But where is Miss Hen? Then I see her—

HIS D
FOR TH
AN OPEN
PACIFIC MO
ME DARLING
ULD BE
ANCING UNDER
DOWN WHERE TH
WINDS BLOW
EAST OF THE SUN
EASTSIDE OF HEAVE
FIESTA
FINESSE
HAWAII CALLS

Chickens go feather-flapping in every direction.

Miss Hen is gone before I even get a good look at her.

Big Mama says you can do anything you put your mind to—if you want it bad enough. I want Miss Hen. I stand watching those chickens, but pretend I'm not.

The chickens watch me, and I watch them. I think all kinds of chicken thoughts so they won't know I'm up to something.

Corn, I think, bright, shiny knuckles of yellow corn.

Eggs! Eggs! Eggs! Goldy-brown eggs all warm, warm, warm.

Corn bread, corn bread! Crumb and crumble bread.

Worms, slurms, swishy-mishy, ickly-tickly worms!

I stand so still even my shadow gets bored and starts to walk off. Just when I'm about to grow feathers, along steps Miss Hen. I peek at her out of the corner of my eye.

Keep still. Keep still and then—

I frog-jump after Miss Hen. Brown legs kicking. Arms flapping and pigtails sailing. Miss Hen goes flying, beak clacking, yellow legs scooting, quick-quick-quick and—gone!

k
K
K
K
K

That chicken got away again. I go and sit by the back step and take a drink from the silver dipper. Chasing chickens is hard work. Seems like, these days, Miss Hen makes herself as hard to find as she is to catch. Where does she hide?

Under the porch in the cool shade? No.

By the well house, scratching for worms? No.

Over by the fishpond peck-pecking for bugs? No.

Where is that hen?

And then I hear it. Over by Big Mama's summer cookstove in the tall, tall grass I hear something soft and low: "Pee-o, pee-o, pee-o." I high-step, high-step, and stand still. I see soft yellow shapes. Molasses-easy, I crouch down low. Molasses-slow, I pull the grass aside.

And there on a nest of brown eggs, with three baby chicks already hatched, sits Miss Hen. So this is where she's been! Miss Hen looks at me steady and hard, her eyes knife-bright, her beak raised like a sharp question. She hunkers down, but she doesn't move.

Miss Hen is so close that my fingers tickle. I know for sure I can snatch her up. My toes start to itch, getting ready to leap. I could do it.

I could snatch her up and run like the wind blowing—I could—I know I could.

But I don't. I look again at those fuzzy chicks cuddling tight beneath her wing. "Pee-o, pee-o, pee-o," they sing.

"Don't you worry, Miss Hen," I say. "I know you're a mama now. You're doing what you need to do. I won't trouble your babies."

Miss Hen settles back into her nest. "Pruck! Pruck! Pruck!" That must be chicken for "Hmpf! That girl's not as bad as I thought!"

Now, every day, Miss Hen goes strutting by like a Fourth of July parade with twelve chicks right behind her! "Peo-peo!" "**Pruck!**" "Peo-peo!" "**Pruck!**" "Peo-peo-peo-peo-peo." "**Pruckkkkkk!**"

PRUCK!

Big Mama says you'd never know I used to be a chicken chaser. It's true! I'm so good, I can't believe it's me. Every morning I throw crushed corn out for Miss Hen and her babies. I catch grasshoppers and dig worms to give to the chicks. I even keep an eye out for chicken-sneaking weasels and egg-sucking snakes. I bet that Ol' Rooster thinks it's too good to be true oo-oo, oo-ooooo!

Big Mama says good things come to those who wait. So I'm waiting for Miss Hen's chicks to grow up, and then I'm going to teach them to run so fast that no one will ever catch them—

not even a chicken chaser like me!

Distributed in Canada by Douglas & McIntyre Ltd.
Color separations by Embassy Graphics
Printed in August 2009 in China by Kwong Fat Offset Printing,
Dongguan City, Guangdong Province
Designed by Barbara Grzeslo
First edition, 2007
9 10 8

www.fsgkidsbooks.com

Library of Congress Cataloging-in-Publication Data
Harrington, Janice N.
The chicken-chasing queen of Lamar County / Janice N. Harrington ; pictures by Shelley Jackson.— 1st ed.
p. cm.
Summary: A young farm girl tries to catch her favorite chicken, until she learns something about the hen that makes her change her ways.
ISBN: 978-0-374-31251-0
[1. Chickens—Fiction. 2. Farm life—Fiction. 3. African Americans—Fiction.] I. Jackson, Shelley, ill. II. Title.

PZ7.H23815 Chi 2007
[E]—dc22

2005052768